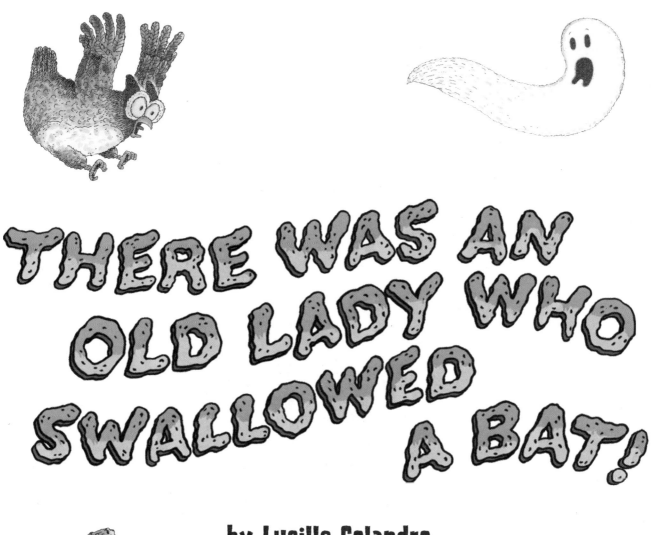

THERE WAS AN OLD LADY WHO SWALLOWED A BAT!

by Lucille Colandro

Illustrated by Jared Lee

Cartwheel BOOKS®

SCHOLASTIC INC.

New York   Toronto   London   Auckland
Sydney   Mexico City   New Delhi   Hong Kong

To my favorite wizards — David and Gene
Love,
L.C.

To my daughter Jana
who loves Halloween
— J.L.

ISBN 978-0-439-73766-1

Text copyright © 2002 by Lucille Santarelli.
Illustrations copyright © 2002 by Jared Lee.
All rights reserved. Published by Scholastic Inc.
SCHOLASTIC, CARTWHEEL BOOKS, and associated logos are trademarks
and/or registered trademarks of Scholastic Inc.

30 29 28 27 26 25 24   16 17/0

Printed in the U.S.A.   40
First printing, September 2002

There was an old lady
who swallowed a bat.
I don't know why she swallowed a bat,
imagine that.

There was an old lady
who swallowed an owl.

My, oh, my, she started to howl.

She swallowed the owl to shush the bat.
I don't know why she swallowed a bat,
imagine that.

There was an old lady
who swallowed a cat.
What do you think? Now she's so fat.

She swallowed the cat to chase the owl.

She swallowed the owl to shush the bat.
I don't know why she swallowed a bat,
imagine that.

There was an old lady
who swallowed a ghost.
What do you think?

She liked it the most!

She swallowed the ghost to catch the cat.
She swallowed the cat to chase the owl.

She swallowed the owl to shush the bat.
I don't know why she swallowed a bat,
imagine that.

There was an old lady
who swallowed a goblin.

It made her so dizzy, she started to spin.

She swallowed the goblin

to scare the ghost.

She swallowed the ghost to catch the cat.

She swallowed the cat to chase the owl.

She swallowed the owl to shush the bat.
I don't know why she swallowed a bat,
imagine that.

There was an old lady
who swallowed some bones.

There were so many, she started to groan.

She swallowed the bones to rattle the goblin.

She swallowed the goblin to scare the ghost.

She swallowed the ghost to catch the cat.

She swallowed the cat to chase the owl.
She swallowed the owl to shush the bat.

I don't know why she swallowed a bat,
imagine that.

There was an old lady
who swallowed a wizard

to cast a spell so she could yell,

"TRICK OR

TREAT!"